Bedard Ishq

Flairs and Glairs
Publication House

"Bedard Ishq"

ISBN No: " 978-93-90416-89-9"
1st Edition
Language – English and Hindi

Flairs and Glairs
Publication House
Regd. Under MSME Act.

-

Disclaimer

Cover Designing
Shubham Shah

Acknowledgement

Dear Almighty, thank you for blessing me with the power and zeal to be able to complete this Anthology. Also, Thank You dear parents, for trusting in me, and letting me work whenever I wanted. My family is the one who supported me for what I am today.
When it comes to this Anthology, I would like to start with Thanking the Co-authors, without your help and support, I would have never been able to complete it.

Thank You all of you, for being there. Much Love to all of You. I am glad to see you all standing by me.

Co Authors

Shubham Shah (Founder Flairs and Glairs)
Ishani Agarwal (Co Founder Flairs and Glairs)
Shivangi Jaiswal (Compiler)

1. Jyoti Singh Rajput
2. Nishiket R Surwade
3. Deepjyoti Chowdhury
4. Heena Shaikh Mulla
5. Shivansh Sharma
6. Shaily Tyagi
7. Nandita Choudhary
8. Ayesha Rajpal
9. Mausam Agrawal
10. Alina Tamkanat
11. Sangeeta Chauhan
12. Hynul Jaseena
13. Shibanee Shataroopa Sahoo
14. Isha
15. Bickey Mandal
16. Piya Kawrani
17. Shijin Ravi C
18. Muskan Gupta
19. Puja Kundu
20. अनिल विश्वकर्मा
21. Parwana Bibi
22. Saloni Lal Srivastava
23. Tathambika
24. Mansi Kanungo
25. Akanksha Sinha

26. Anisha Panda
27. Shresth Bhargava (Yash)
28. Mohua Chakraborty
29. पुलिन भारती
30. Shristi Singh
31. Aditi Vinod Patil
32. Shobha Rajpal
33. Smriti Kumari
34. Pragya Verma
35. Sachin Banoudhiya
36. Arijit Mondal
37. Oke Damilola Deborah
38. Mihika Saraf
39. Vishal Agrawal
40. Sanya Khanna
41. Neha Singhania
42. Aditya Srivastava
43. Chirag L Sagar
44. Maitreyee
45. Soumya Nema
46. Tushar Sachdeva
47. Tusar Ranjan Mahapatra
48. Bushra Shaikh
49. Dr. Ruchita Chauhan
50. Saheb Ghosh

Shubham Shah

(Founder- Flairs and Glairs)

Shubham Shah, entrepreneur at "Flairs & Glairs" a brand with dynamics in events organizing and cultural educational pan INDIA, He is a 26yr. old guy who recently has entered, the digital platform of imprinting emotions. He has initiated with his own open mic platform to help budding poets and aspiring writers under his brand named as "Teekhe Zasbaaat"
He is a commerce graduate from Bhagalpur City of Bihar.
He says Writing has impersonated him since childhood and he has now been writing for over a decade!
Cooking, on the other hand, is his passion! He also mentions, trying out new things just tickles him!
When asked sir, Why SPICY EMOTIONS?

He smiled and added, “agar jasbaat teekhe na ho toh wo jasbaat kaha” Spices are all that blends! So do his words!
As a chef, he presents to you his dish! Hot and freshly served! Taste it! Feel it! Enjoy it! You can also find his writing in the Solo book “Teekhe Zasbaaat” and 70+ anthologies. With his passion to explore opportunities across Platforms he is working with keen devotion and We wish him all the very best for his future ventures
Share your reviews on his

INSTAGRAM

@spicy_emotions
@shubham4shah

Or via email on

shubham2shah@gmail.com

To stay tuned to his work and opportunities follow his business Handles

INSTAGRAM FACEBOOK YOUTUBE

@flairsandglairs
@teekhezasbaaat

WEBSITE:

https://flairsandglairs.in/
https://flairsandglairs.com/

Ishani Agarwal

(Co Founder- Flairs and Glairs)

Ishani Agarwal
Born and brought up in Kolkata, she has done her schooling and college from here itself. She is doing her post-graduation at the moment. Ishani loves talking to people around, and is excited for this new beginning of hers! Been a Compiler for 35+ Anthologies, and in the process for more, also, co-authored in 100+ Anthologies, Ishani is very Happy with how her life is turning out now!
Insta handle: Ishani_agarwal_quotes

Shivangi Jaiswal

(Compiler)

Shivangi Jaiswal is a Content Writer from Kolkata. Project Head & Coordinator at “Flairs & Glairs” brand with dynamics in events organizing and cultural educational pan INDIA. Organiser at "The Glittering Fables" Writing Community. She is a B.Com Honours graduate. Certified in Stocks & Short Selling as well as Certified in Digital Marketing Been a keen student, she has recently been Certified for learning Spanish Language..She loves to bring smiles and happiness to many faces, so she is into social service. Shivangi has also done her

Diploma in painting, drawing and all kinds of clay making, craft works. Traveler, Teacher, Meditator, Dancer, Singer, Instrument Player. She loves to play guitar and harmonium. Been a public speaker she has taken part in many events and nailed it. Also been a great Advisor to many. Sports freak of Swimming and Badminton with a passion so strong. Since, past one year she has started her writing journey. She writes so that many people can connect with their stories and get positive hopes. She thinks " Every story is unique so embrace yourself to the best".She is a writer by day and a reader by night. Been a Complier of 20+ Anthologies, and in process for more, also Co- authored 60+ anthologies. Shivangi is an old soul with young eyes, a vintage heart, and a beautiful mind."

You can follow her work:

Instagram

@the_knockingvibe

@house_of_compilations

Why?

Awaking up all night,
Wishing of things to change.
I try to calm myself, trying to heal,
Throwing away all the heaviness.
All I need is a comfortable sleep.

Broken, shattered all I was,
Just waiting for a sign of hope.
Watching myself dying every day,
But so much hurt
I couldn't stay.

You pushed me to the point of breaking
Played with my heart,
Ruined my life
Never turned back
And left all things unsaid.

Why did you break?
Why did you leave?
Was breaking me was your happiness?
Was leaving me in mid-way was right?
Why did you break me?
Why? So many answers are left behind.

I'm Lost Completely.

I'm lost completely.
Not knowing how to mend my heart
Not knowing how to fix my broken pieces.
Not knowing how will I be fine.
Not knowing will ever be things all right.

My mind is overflowing with memories of you,
that we shared together.
My dreams are broken with a touch.
My heart doesn't know what to do.

How do I find hope?
How do I find a new way of life?
How do I believe now?
How do I even trust anyone?

Blinded in fear.
I'm drowning now.
I'm struggling to come out.
Not knowing what will happen next.
Hoping for a way out.

You Tore Me..

From stealing by heart
To breaking me apart.
You did all that you want.

From giving false hopes
To lying each and every day.
You made me lose trust from all.

From loving me,
To making my heart shattered into pieces.
You played well by wearing a mask of a
second face.

From forever promises,
To fake promises.
You burned me upon fire.

From being the perfect one,
To be the game player.
You showed all your true colors by time.

From living in the present and loving my future.
To dwelling for lifetime.
You gave me a goodbye all I could think of "Why?"

Fake Smile

I wear a smile,
which is empty inside.
Leaving it back behind the past.
Not knowing about the future.

Crying inside,
But no one could see my tears.
All I wanted was you near me.
But I feel I'm tied up with chains
Trapped all around in a box
Not knowing the way out to go.

It's painful
It's hurtful
It's tearing me inside
It's killing me.
I need you to be here with me.

This pain is taking over all.
But my love for you will never get old.
A painful misery keeps on going.
From love to pain.
I will always be painfully in love with you
.

Jyoti Singh Rajput

Jyoti Singh Rajput is a banker by profession and marks the ink, as her passion. She believes, the pen holded with passion, has power to bring change and it even emote the emotions, that can't be verbally exchanged and are left unsaid. She is also a lyricist, a nature lover, an enthusiast contributing to welfare works and urges all to help those who needs, as she says, we are human for good deeds. A multilingual and a promising poet, Jyoti Singh Rajput has worked in many books of different genres. She is a basket of masterpieces and her poetry sheds stories, some of love and the memories, some of those tinch and the waving worries, some of life and it's theories. You can follow her on instagram @ the_frozen_flame_2801, and on yourquote @ Jyoti - the frozen flame for her more write ups.

ये इश्क और ये आशिकी

हर नूरे नज़र का जाम पिया करते हो
नये चाँद का दीदार कई शाम किया करते हो
एहसासों की आजमाइश बार-बार किया करते हो
फिर मोहब्बत के नाम पर
हमें क्यूँ बदनाम किया करते हो
क्यूँ हमारे इकरार का इंतज़ार किया करते हो
क्यूँ हमें अपने इश्क का उनवान दिया करते हो
जब गैरों से आशिकी सरेआम किया करते हो..

Nishiket R Surwade

Mr.Nishiket R Surwade,born on 24th July 1999 .He is a student pursuing his engineering in electronics and telecommunication field ,Nashik, Maharashtra. He is very shy and simple, easily make friends.He is a blogger and future E&TC engineer. He aspires to become IAS Officer. He started writing as a career since he was in 12th St. He loves to write quote and shayri in Hindi as well as in English language. He loves to write about 'True love ‘He worked as co-author in some anthologies like 'The Broken Bond','For the name of love' and in more than 35 Anthologies. and also Being a compiler of the book "College Romance" ,"Life Sahi Hai" and many are in process

Tuta Dil Hai Hamara.

Tuta hai dil hamara is main aapki kya galti,

Galti to hamari hai humne aapko chaha.

Zakham to milna hi tha ,

Khud ko dard dene ka shauk jo hai humain tha.

Ummid bhi humne unse ki,

Jinhe hamare hone ka ahsaas tak nahi tha.

Fursat kaha hai kisi ko iss tute dil

Ka haal sunne ke liye.

Isliye dard sine main liye ,

Jhuthi muskurahat rakhna jaruri tha.

Ab tut gaya hai sukh aur dukh ka fasla ,

Isliye apno ki khusi ke liye lena pada humain ,

Jhuthi hasi ka sahara....

(2)

Maine kabhi kisi ko todna na chaha ,

Tumhe kabhi kisi ko jodna na chaha.

Ab akela tutkar kanch ke tukdon ki,

Tarah bikhar chuka hoon.

(3)

Kitna ajib hai naa

Ankhein samndar nahin

Phir bhi bhar aati hai

Aur dil kanch kaa nahin

Phir bhi tut jata hai....

(4)

Tum kya samjhoge mohabbat ko

Khud ke tut jane par bhi kisi ko

Chahna aasan nahin hota...

Deepjyoti Chowdhury

Deepjyoti Chowdhury embraces reading and writing as her escape from the real world as well as a window to it. She is a strong believer of Christ and Karma. Written in 100+ anthologies, she is the author of "Heartfelt musings" and "The staircase to freedom". Her main aim is to heal people and make them smile through her art of writing. You can follow her on Instagram at dj_writes_to_heal .

LOVE HURTS AND LOVE HEALS

Dear readers,

Today if you're concerned about that hurtful feeling that still recides in your soul, I want to tell you that let the pain dissolve in your soul. That wound is deep I know, but it hurts only when we make an effort in touching the wound. Stop touching it and let it heal on it's own. Give it time and space for healing. Every hurt is building you to turn into what you're meant to be. Every tear you're shedding will be worth it. Even if no one acknowledges, the universe knows every bit of the pain and misery you've been through. The secret is that, just like love has hurted you, love will heal you. It might not be the same person but the healing will be divine and you would be thankful to the Almighty that the person who was killing you from within was thrown out of your life with a purpose just at the right time. Don't question the universe why me? Be cheerful that it is you. A misery is brought to our table only when we are capable enough of facing it. The love that you thought was the most amazing feeling then, do not let those memories become toxic. Cherish the good memories and let those lessons be carved in your soul forever. Be a better you and keep smiling because if you're reading this, you're courageous enough! Trust yourself.

From your healer and writer,

Heena Shaikh Mulla

Heena Shaikh Mulla is from Pune,currently residing in Karnataka.

She's from an ICSE background,graduated from Pune University(MSC Computer Science). She's the author of 'Technical Desserts' and also hold a Vajra record for the same. Besides being a college topper,She likes drawing henna,teaching and fantasizes about Polar Bears.

She's a charming personality who expresses her thoughts in the form of Poetry and Shayri and currently she's compiling books as well.

Khamoshi Ki Aawaz

Jo samaj jaye khamoshi ka raaz,
Vo karta hai sab par raaj.

Jaha samaj naa aaye jawab,
Vaha khamosh rehana hai la-jawab.

Jo baat keh kar naa samjhai jaaye,
Vo haqikat agar khamosh rehane se samne aaye.

Iska swaad hai bada meetha,
Jo chake vo kadwahat bhool jaye.

Bhale hi khamoshi ki aawaz nahi hoti,
Par usse bade bade buniyade hil jati hai.

Bina teer chalaye,
Khamoshi sabko cheer jati hai.

Shivansh Sharma

He is shivansh sharma . Basically from indore but persuing MBA(Marketing &Hr) in mysore karnataka . He always have passion towards writng the thoughts which comes in to his mind . A hardcore fodiee as he belongs to indore . He is the one who is always ready to help to his near ones .His life revolves around his family and friends. He is always self motivated , enthusiastic and person with positive vibes .He is co-author of 10+ books and compiler of 1 book . His only belief is just live happily and enjoy every moment of life .
You can contact him on ig@shivanshrockzzzzz

इंतकाम

ख्वाबो मे तुम खयालों मे तुम
लेकिन अफसोस ख्याल-ए-दिल,
तुम कही नहीं,
आंखे ढूंढती हे पल - पल
लेकिन तुम हो गए हो ओझल,
टूटा हुआ साज हू मैं
खुद से ही नाराज़ हू मैं ,
क्या तूने मुझे खो दिया हे
या खुदसे बर्बाद हु मैं ,
एक बात पूछता हू
तुमसे हमदम जब जाना ही था
तो आई क्यो,
जीना मेरा खुशहाल कर तू मिल कर
ये एहसान कर याद तेरी सताती हे,
नींद एक पल ना अति हे
जैसे गिर पड़े हो बदल मुझ पर
आह दिल मे रहे जाति हे,
शायद अब कभी ना मिलेगी
हमे वो प्यार की मंज़िल
जिसके लिए बने थे हम मुसाफिर,
बहुत रोका समझाया मनाया लेकिन
तुमने ना एक सुनी ना तरस खाया,
जो भी कसमें खाईं थी
तुमने वादा किये थे जो
तुमने एक भी ना निभा पाए तुम लोट कर भी ना आपाए,

जो गए हो तो अब आना ही मत
अपनी बेवफ़ाई ओर हम पर बरसाना मत,
तेरी रुसवाई भी भूल जाएंगे,
कुछ नया करके इतिहास रच जाएंगे
आशिको मे नाम कर जाएंगे।

Shaily Tyagi

She is Shaily Tyagi, a born writer.
She is always ready to face challenges and gives her best in every field.
She is a compiler, loves to compile different feelings of different hearts.
Here she is with her beautiful poem, hope all will love to read.

प्यार कैसा

भुला दूं तुझे एक भूल सा,
तो फिर वह प्यार कैसा,
हंसते लबों की चुभन को,
जो ना समझ सके,
तो फिर वह यार कैसा।
अगर गुजर सके सुकून का एक भी पल तेरे बिना,
तो फिर मैं बेकरार कैसा।
कफन तक ना साथ ले चलू,
वह तेरे मिलने की खुशबू,
तो फिर वह इंतजार कैसा।
कहना पड़े अगर लबों से,
बिन कुछ कहे ना समझ सके,
तो फिर यह इजहार कैसा।
भुला दूं तुझे एक फूल सा तो फिर वो प्यार कैसा।

Nandita Choudhary

Nandita, as her name signifies “The one who pleases”, a survivor of hatred and pain. Her poems, her writings are a beautiful mixture of love, struggles, and pain.If you are looking of something really lovely, having real pain & real beauty in living, Nandita has got gems for you.

Raindrops

One after another,
The raindrops race each other.
Two Side by side,
On the window they continue to slide.
Three is one too much,
So close to each other, they touch.
Four is too crowded,
With raindrops my vision is enshrouded.
Five covers my fears,
As the raindrops mix with my tears.
Six requires an umbrella,
While my depression begins its acappella.
Seven is the jackpot,
Through which my sanity and depression crackpot.
Eight raindrop is great,
I'm leaving it all on my fate.
Nine is where I see a reflection,
Trying to ask me a question.
Ten is not my expectation,
Not my salvation.
One by one,
I'm left undone

Angels Of The Heaven

The sea was clam
The world was blind
To see the cries
Of the heavenly lives.
Molestation
Exploitation
Making them feel Broken
For the things they thought
would change human
Made them the Lucifer of Earth.
How cruel the world is changing to be.
How the ones who brought them to this world
Are nothing in front of money.
How a woman is nothing
But a doll to take out rage.
How feelings are nothing
In front of lust.
Is this what we call development
The angels are crying
Seeing how we are turning out to be.

Ayesha Rajpal

Ayesha Rajpal is writer by passion. She is into nobel profession of teaching and runs an academy in Delhi. She is fun lovung and easy going person and has been co author for few books . She is into writing poems . Even she loves calligraphy and Mandala art too.

Bewafa

Na jaana humne kya gustakhi ki thi
Humne socha ki sbne milane ki koshish ki thi
Pta na tha ki tum yu chor jaaooge
Aur tanha is tarah chor ke muh mor jaooge
Chaht thi tumhe srf paane ki
Na pta tha ki aise dur chle jaaoge
Umeed thi ki tum wapas aooge
Pr hum to wahin h jahan chorda tha apne
Pr kya pta tha tum khin dur Nikal jaooge

Mausam Agrawal

She is 22 year old girl from Nepal and is currently pursuing C.A. She loves writing poems,stories ,shayaris and twoliners

Bas Abh Nahi Intezaar Tera

Yun toh ishq humne bhi kiya hai
Bas abh uske charche nahi karte
Jisko kabhi sanam mana tha
Bas aaj kal hum uspe nahi marte

Bade sabar se raah takte hai unke liye
Khud ko bhula kar unki khusiyon ki duayein mangi thi
Par guzar gaya woh waqt
Woh insaan abh dil se utar gaya
Jisse kabhi ki thi mohbbat
Woh insaan hi badal gaya...

Write-up 2 with Title
Sukoon paya hai saalon baad
Bhula kar unko
Jaise kisi kaed se nikle ho
Ki marte the jinki khusiyon ke khatir
Abh unke khayalon se bhi ruswai nibhayi hai
Tasavur mai jinki shamein bitayi thi kayi
Najaane kitni raaton ko needin gawayi thi
Abh khud se mohbbat ki toh jana
Ki zaarort kabhi thi hi nahi unke sath ki

Alina Tamkanat

Hello friends
It's me Alina tamkanat
I like to see Dreams in an open eyes and then I like to work on them to fulfill it..
I'm passionate for facing camera for acting,modelling and for holding camera making new new videos and vlogs ..and I make my leg tired by traveling..
But my hobbies are to relaxing my eyes by reading some good books and moving my hand with my pen for writing some stories and shayiris
So, I work both of them. I follow my passion and work on my hobbies...
For improving my self and make better version of me.
Thank you....

Mohabbat Chhod Denge Hum...

..Sapne dikha kyon tor diya, Waada kar sath nibhane ka Manzil se pahle hi kyon chhod diya, Ab tujhse sare ristey tod denge hum, Mohabbat chhod denge hum, Mohabbat chhod denge hum... Ab to akele rahne ki aadat si hain , hain, Tujhse to mujhe ab nafrat Kisi ko ab apna dil na denge hum, Mohabbat chhod denge hum, mohabbat chhod denge hum, Tune mujhe aisa thokar mara ki muskurana bhi bhul gyi hoon, Apne dard ko hi pyar samajh rahi hoon, Ab tere pyar se bhi mu'h mor lenge hum, Mohabbat chhod denge hum, mohabbat chhod denge hum. .

Sangeeta Chauhan

She is Sangeeta Chauhan from Mumbai,Maharashtra she loves to write what she feels from heart ,you can check her write-ups on instagram her id is _.creative_quotes._

(1)

Ek Aansoon bol pada
Na Jane kitne raaz khol pada,
Dil bhara bhara sa tha...
Aaj unko halka Karne ke liye,
Jii bhar ke ro pada...
Ek Aansoon bol pada
Na jane kitne raaz khol pada....

(2)

सब कुछ छूट रहा था
और यह दिल भी टूट रहा था
आँखें नम सी हो गई थी
के यह राते भी नहीं बीत रही थी
यह घर भी वीरान सी लग रही थी
मनो कोई रहता ही नहीं ऐसा महसूस हो रहा था
सब कुछ छूट रहा था
और यह दिल भी टूट रहा था
अकेले ही दिन गुज़रता था
दिन रात यादो में पल बितता
मनो समय भी हमसे रूठ रहा था
सब कुछ छूट रहा था
और यह दिल भी टूट रहा था
दिल की बाते भी करे तो किससे करे
अंदर ही अंदर दम घुट रहा था
सब कुछ छूट रहा था
और यह दिल भी टूट रहा था

Hynul Jaseena

This is Miss. Hynul Jaseena.
She is a teacher by profession and a resident of Mysore, Karnataka.
She loves to read and write.
Her passion of becoming a writer is still a blazing fire.
She has written many thoughts and quotes on life.
Do follow her official Instagram page @binte_sadakath for more such quotes.

The Unmatched Love

I was a midnight chime,
You were on bed at early time.
I would leave my stomach to be tight,
You are a person of good apetite.
I dreamt of Romeo,
You were Sherlock Holmes.
I loved the winter nights in hamlets,
You loved the busy metro in NY.
I wished to get immersed in drizzles,
You were a fitness freak.
I laughed my heart out,
You showed even your smile is costly.
I showed the life is to love,
You believed the life is to live.
I enjoyed the cozy quilts,
You'd set foot of floors.
I loved to drench in slight pour,
You would search for shelter.
I just wanted your mere time,
You gave the reasons meantime.
I wanted to build our future together
You wanted to make the world better.
I always wanted a simple 'love you',
You did give me a 'will call you'.
I wanted to walk together
But
You ran alone

Shibanee Shataroopa Sahoo

A free flirtatious soul beneath the deep, blue, sky.
Yun toh Shayar nahi hai hum
Baas dil ki baatein zuban pe na lake kalam pe late hain hum.
She is Shibanee Shataroopa Sahoo and her words flows from her heart.

Rooh Ki Aansoon

Aansuon ki bhasa
Bahut gehri hai zanab
Inhe samjh ne ke liye ankhe kafi nahi
Mohabbat chahiye
Dil ankhon me dastak deti hai
Aur rooh kisi apnoko !!

Fareb Ishq

Dil ne ki thi Gustakhi
Kar betha tumse Ishq
Uss bechare ko kya pata tha
Tumhe Ishq hai Gairon se
Chah kar bhi tumhare wo Ehsaas
Ko na bhula sake
Wo jhute KASME ko bechara Hakeekat maan baitha tha
Tumhare Fareb ishq ko bhi Masoomiyat samjh kar Apna liya tha
Dil ne ki thi gustakhi
Ishq Kiya Tha Tumse

Isha

A warrior with a warm heart who is ready to fight every situation fearlessly. She is a poet, a writer, a lyricist, and a Shayar, all-in-one. She has been writing since she was a kid. It is as if writing is in her blood and creativity flows in her veins. A girl with a passion for writing, and a curious soul who wants to fly in an open sky using her words. She is an Assistant Manager for Social Media & Online Reputation Management by profession who holds a Masters Degree in English. She feels that love is the best feeling one can ever experience in life. Her family and friends are her strength. She marks her presence on Instagram @virtuous_soul17 which is her personal account, whereas she posts all her writings @pristinetales on Instagram.

We hope you will enjoy her creative work. Happy Reading!

इश्क़ आज भी है

इश्क़ भले ही मुकम्मल ना हुआ मेरा,
पर यादों में वो मेरी आज भी है।
मेरी ज़िंदगी का हिस्सा वो भले ही ना रहा,
पर दुआओं में शामिल वो आज भी है।
यादें मिटती नहीं महज़ तस्वीरें मिटा देने से,
उसका वो हंसता हुआ चेहरा नज़र में आज भी है,
मगर उसके साथ रहने की तमन्ना नहीं अब दिल में,
उसका वो बेरुखा बर्ताव मुझे याद आज भी है।
मांगती हूं आज भी हर पल उसकी खुशी इबादत में,
हम दूर भले ही हैं पर इश्क़ मुझे आज भी है।।

इश्क़ - एक बवंडर

इश्क़ वो बवंडर है, जिसमें तू तबाह होगा,
ए दिल संभल जा,
वरना खामाखा इश्क़ में फनाह होगा।
इस बेदर्द इश्क़ ने दर्द सभी को दिया है,
कोई इश्क़ कर के रोया है,
कोई खुद को गवा के रोया है।।

Bickey Mandal

He is Bickey Mandal from Jharkhand. Now he is in the last semester of his graduation from B.B.M.K.U Dhanbad with English Honours. With his poetries he trying to connect himself with others. He is passionate about his works because he love what he do. He have a stedy source of motivations that drives him to do his best. He wants to became a writer from last 5 year so, he collect his Thoughts, Poetry and Lyrics from then to make a good book in his both books he presenting many beautiful shayari, Love quotes , Motivational quotes & sad stories. You can contact him through instagram at @bickey_ki_ankahi_baatein

E-mail- bickeymandal91@gmail.com

I Scared Of You

I can't imagine my life without you .
Because I want to hold your hand tightly,
When I scared.
I am not good enough,
But even I am not too bad.

I think I am happy without you.
But I can't be happy,
because I am happy only with you.
You don't leave me I will be who,
You want me to be.

I can't forgive you,
But forget you.
And regret myself,
For my mistakes.

Piya Kawrani

Piya kawrani was born in Godhra (Gujarat) and later she got married with Vinay Kawrani in Ahmedabad.
She has done MBA . She was in writing from long back , and considered words as her bestfriend. We can say , she actually express the actual meaning of words with her writing skills. We all were in shocked when we come to know that she writes so well as she is of jolly nature and believes in spreading smile in her surroundings .
She loves listening music and travelling .

(1)

एक पल था जब हम तुम्हारी चुप्पी भी समज जाते थे
जब हँसकर सब भुला देते थे
जब निगाहों से ही बात कर लिया करते थे
जब तुम्हारे सामने आते ही सब कुछ थम सा जाता था
तुमसे ही थी सब बाते
कुछ अधूरी तो कुछ पूरी
कुछ लम्हे अब भी याद आते है
कुछ अधूरी सी बातें पूरी करने का जी चाहता है
तुमसे शुरू हुई इस कहानी को तुमसे ही खत्म करने को जी चाहता है
तुझमे ही बस जाना है
तुझमे ही खो जाना है
वक्त का पता नही, नाही ज़िन्दगी का
तुम अगर आ पाओ तो अभ भी आ जाओ
में वही खड़ी हु जहा छोड़ गए थे।

(2)

वक्त रहते साथ निभाया होता
हाथो को यू छोड़ा न होता
कुछ और ही मांगती है जिंदगी अब हमसे
तुमसे बिछड़ने का गम पाया न होता
अब तो तुम्हारी कमी कुछ इस तरह खलती है कि न दिन का पता
चलता है ना रात का
बस युही वक्त बीत रहा
ना कोई उम्मीद
ना कोई अहसास
ना किसी से बात
ना ही तकरार
बस ज़िन्दगी है तो जीनी है
वरना अब मौत का भी इंतज़ार ना रहा।

Shijin Ravi C

He is Mr. Shijin Ravi C from Kerala.He is pursuing BSc Hons Agriculture graduate.He is a young poet and co-author of many anthologies today. Some of his anthologies are 'The golden words','The uncertain periods','My success ladder','Safar','Her voice','Positive vibes' etc .His mail ID is shijinravi23@gmail.com . His Instagram ID is stolen.pearl .

The Little Flower

I knew her quiet well from childhood,
Like from we did played and shared hours,
But never did I had a love for her,
That as days become too old this moment,
My heart just beats for her soul.

She have grown from now to a pearl,
Admiring all the fellows near by ,
To the most beautiful lady I have ever seen,
She was the talk of the crowd,
With flowers crowning her curly hairs.

I was in crush with her arrival,
For the first time in my whole life,
Where I felt everyone around me like her,
Dancing and singing with the flow,
Taking me away from myself along.

Like the fountain to watch she was the star,
She was my sun and moon in travel,
My life was flying so well that time,
Atlast without a twist she was all mine,
My wife and friend to all my success.

Muskan Gupta

She is Muskan Gupta ,lives in Ayodhya, Uttar Pradesh. She is a student and doing graduation from Delhi University. She have a keen interest in writing poetries, stories ,quotes, rants and shayaris and loves to express her feelings in words. She have a burning desire to achieve her aim &want to explore in the field of writing .Recently, she worked as a co-author for more then ten books .

Thus, she want to inspire people by her writings.

Yaadein Teri,Baatein Teri .

Yaadein teri,baatein teri ..saari mulakaatein teri ..
Chehrey par muskurahat teri .. aur neendo mein woh baatein teri ..
Bus yaadein teri baatein teri... saari mulakaatein teri...
Kuch ashqon mein chipey dard tere... woh roshini si chamak teri ..
Bus yaadein, teri baatein teri... saari mulakaatein teri
Khud ki gustaakiyan teri... khud ki badmasshiyan teri... khud pr krodh aur khud par Khushi Teri ..in hi baaton ko bayaan Karta hai...Ki...
Yaadein teri ,baatein teri ...saari mulakaatein teri... Tujhe aaj bhi uski Yaad dilaati hai.

"Zaroori toh Nahi"

Kuch baatein poori ho yeh bhi zaroori toh nahi...
Kuch rishtey anmol ho yeh bhi toh zaroori nahi...
Kuch raaste manzil se jurey ho yeh zaroori toh nahi...
Kuch khwahisey muqkamal naa ho yeh bhi toh zaroori nahi...
Kuch jazbaat dilon ki chaadar mein simtey ho yeh bhi toh zaroori nahi...
Kai logo ke pyaar mohobbat ho yeh bhi toh zaroori nahi...

Puja Kundu

MBBS STUDENT, BUDDING AUTHOR.

" ख़्वाब या हक़ीक़त? "

मेरे लिये कौन हो तुम?
हक़ीक़त या ख़्वाब,
या कोई आंकही राज़ हो तुम?
कभी हासील ना हो सका वो खुबसूरत एहसास हो तुम..
इन साँसों के लिये , ज़रूरत नहीं, बेहध ज़रूरी हो तुम,
चाहत नहीं, इबादत हो तुम..
गरमी की वो धूप जैसी, सर्द की वो दोपहेर् हो तूम,
बारीश की वो बूँद जैसी, सवान् की वो मेहक हो तूम,
नफ़रत नहीं, नाराज़गी है तूमसे,
शिकायात् नहीं, बेपनाह मोहब्बत है तूमसे,
सिर्फ अल्फ़ाज़ नहीं, मेरी खामोशी भी तूम,
सिर्फ खयालात् नहीं, मेरी हक़ीक़त भी तूम..
मेरे शुभः में तूम, मेरे शामों में तूम
मेरे जेहेन्-ओ-जहान् में भी तूम,
बस मेरे बस में नहीं हों तुम।

अनिल विश्वकर्मा

लेखक को श्री अनिल कुमार विश्वकर्मा के नाम से जाना जाता है, वे देश की राजधानी दिल्ली से सम्बन्ध रखते हैं। उनकी स्नातक की शिक्षा दिल्ली विश्वविद्यालय से हुई है तथा वर्तमान में वे एक प्रतिष्ठित संगठन में कार्यरत हैं। वे एक गम्भीर व ज़िम्मेदार युवक होने के साथ-साथ कर्तव्यनिष्ठ और पारिवारिक व्यक्ति भी हैं। अपने जीवन के दैनिक कार्यों में व्यस्त रहते हुए भी वे अपनी लेखन रुचि को जीवित रखते हैं। अपने स्नातकोत्तर के दौरान ही उनमें लेखन की रुचि उत्पन्न हो गई थी, किंतु इस कला को भौतिक स्वरूप देने में उन्हें कुछ समय लगा। उनके लेखन की प्रेरणा व स्रोत उनकी प्रिय जीवनसंगिनी है। वे थोड़े अल्पभाषी है किंतु कलम के माध्यम से वे अपनी बात कहना जानते हैं। वे अपनी रचनाओं और लेखनी के माध्यम से आप लोगों से जुड़ना चाहते हैं तथा साथ ही साथ यह भी कामना करते हैं कि आप लोगों का प्रोत्साहन व स्नेह भी उन्हें भरपूर मिले क्योंकि वे इस क्षेत्र में अभी नवीन हैं परंतु इस यात्रा में और आगे तक जाने की इच्छा रखते हैं।

गुबार।

होता है क्यों ऐसा, मानता हूँ जिसे अपना,
वही मेरी बातों को, जरा भी नहीं समझता।
हो जाता है ख़फ़ा, जरा सी बात पर वो,
क्या उसके सीने में, अब वो दिल नहीं धड़कता।

निकालके रख देता हूँ, सीने से अपने दिल को,
पर इस बात से, अब उसे कोई फर्क नहीं है पड़ता।
चिंगारी ही काफ़ी है, ठंडी आग को बस,
वो कुछ बोल दे तो, फिर मैं भी नहीं सम्भलता।

आ जाता है बवंडर, इस दिल के समंदर में,
ग़र हद से वो बढ़ जाए, तो मैं भी नहीं ठहरता।
हालातों में ऐसे, दिल अक्सर बहुत है रोता,
धोके-बाज़ों का, दोबारा हाथ मैं भी नहीं पकड़ता।

बेचैन कर देती है, वो सारी तमाम यादें,
सारी रात अगर वो रोये, इधर मैं भी हूँ तड़पता।
चुभ जातें हैं कुछ तीर, एक दुसरे को,
ग़र मुझसे वो है लड़ते, तो मैं भी क्यों हूँ झगड़ता।

दोबारा नहीं हो सकता।

चला गया हो जो दूर रूठ-कर हमसे, क्या वो फिर हमारा नहीं हो सकता।

ठुकरा दिया हो सबने जिसको, क्या उसका कोई सहारा नहीं हो सकता।

रिश्ता आफ़ताब का महज़ एक जुगनू से, इस दुनिया को गंवारा नहीं हो सकता।

ता-उम्र किसी का साथ देने के बाद, क्या कोई फिर से कंवारा नहीं हो सकता।

टूट जाये जो किसी कश्ती की पतवार, क्या उसका कोई किनारा नहीं हो सकता।

दिल्लगी कर बैठे जो किसी भी हसीं से, ऐसा हर शख़्स आवारा नहीं हो सकता।

एकबार ख़ामोश होने के बाद कोई सैलाब, क्या उफ़न फिर दोबारा नहीं सकता।

गलत कहते हैं सब की एक बार होने के बाद, प्यार फिर दोबारा नहीं हो सकता।

Parwana Bibi

Parwana Bibi a little moody and shy girl .She want to see people happy and she is so cute .And she is very talented and never give up any situation .Let's see what she write for us.

Bedard Ishq Yeh Tera

Julm kamaya hai humne bedard si teri iss ishq mein ...
Zalim to log hain lekin daag lagate hain mohabbat mein...
Humne to jeena chaha thha sath tumhare .....
Per tumne to suli pe chadhane ka soch rakha thha mujhe......

Raha Nazar Na Aaye

Tut ke bikhar gaya hai yeh dil jaise kadak ke bijli kahin giri ho,
Uda le gaya hai sari khusiyan jaise hawayen andhi ko...

Sari ummidein mit chuki hai jaise janam janam ki yadein,
Kho gaya hai sara manzil jaise behete paniyon ki leherein...

Saloni Lal Srivastava

She is Saloni Lal Srivastava daughter of Mr. Kumar Prashant and Mrs. Asha Sinha from Siwan, Bihar. She is a girl from a small town with her big dreams. Her life is all around her family, friends and career. In present she is purchasing B.sc in Botany hounors. She work as co author in 25+ anthologies. She is one of those who love to spread smile and positivity to everyone. Her instagram handle is @salonilalsrivastava.

मेरी क्या गलती थी

जिंदगी तू ही बता
मेरी क्या गलती थी
उससे बेइंतहा मोहब्बत की
क्या यही मेरी गलती थी
जिंदगी तू ही बता
मेरी क्या गलती थी
उसे अपनी जिंदगी बना ली
क्या यही मेरी गलती थी
जिंदगी तू ही बता
मेरी क्या गलती थी

रात और उसकी याद

हर रात चुपके-चुपके
याद तेरी आ जाती है
कितना भी बहलालू
इस पागल दिल को
आंख फिर भी भर आती है
नादान है ये दिल
चाह कर भी तुझे भुला नहीं पाता है
हर रात चुपके-चुपके
बस ये दिल असकों में डूब जाता है
Write-up 3 with Title
वह एक दफ़ा कह कर देखें तो सही,
उनकी खुशी की ख़ातिर खुद को बदलना मंजूर है हमें,
पर अफ़सोस हमसे बातें करना भी नामंजूर है उन्हें।

Tathambika

I m a simple girl with big dreams !
I just express what I feel
Add I am a mba scholar & live in Dhanbad Jharkhand
I'd- tathu895(crazy thoughts)

Bedard Ishq

Zindagi jakham ki tasweer banke reh gya , tu mere dil pae lggi tir banke reh gya , Bedard jamane ka ke tano ko sunte sunte, ye tamasha meri takdeer banke reh gya ...
Tumhara aana, hame khwab dikhana, or khwaabon ko adhura chorkr chale jana theek tha kya?
Jeete jee shikwae geele karte rhe , dosto k samne jhuta pyar jatana theek tha kya?
Shikhaya to bht kch h tumne or zindagi ne
Shikhaya to bht h tumhare khayalon ne,
shikhaya to bht h tumhare badalte vyavahaaroin ne, tumhare najarandaj karne k tarikon ne,
Sikhaya to bht h tumhare vapas aane ki umeedoin ne...
Ek saheed bete k dard se maloom para mujhe ki mera dard ko bht kam h ,
Arsha beet gaye seene se lage tere, mera naseeb vi to dekho lauta vi to saheed hoke dar pae tere!
Dard ko tum seh lena mere dost , Zindagi tumhe bht mauke degi...

Mansi Kanungo

मेरा नाम मानसी कानूनगो है, मैं इंदौर (मध्यप्रदेश) से हूं। मैं 19 वर्ष की हूं , लिखना मेरा पेशा नहीं मेरी आदत है।

(1)

तक़दीर में शायद तु नहीं बस तेरी यादें हैं,
और तेरे दूर होने के हज़ार झूठे इरादे है,
तेरे प्यार में कई शामे मेंनै गुज़ार दी....
क्योंकि अब तु नहीं बस मेरे पास तेरी बेवफ़ाई के बहूत सारे झूठे वादे है।

(2)

मेरे टुटे ख़्वाब सही,
बिखरे जस्बात सही,
चल अब मान भी लिया कि मैं ही गलत हु
तु और तेरे हालात सही....।

(3)

कि मैं तेरे हर सवाल का जवाब दूंगी।
तु मिल तो मैं मेरे हर किस्से का हिसाब लूंगी

Akanksha Sinha

Akanksha Sinha is student by profession ,writer as passion. Lives in Patna,Bihar. She loves to portrait feelings by her poetry and quotes,she likes travelling and capturing moments. Heart healer by birth. She is co author of 15+ anthology. She loves to feel the nature. She is passionate &ambitious for her work.

Currently, she is been a co-author in several anthologies and compiling her first anthology named "Zindagi-Ek-Ehsaas"... She has own page namely " @merelabzz " on Instagram.

टूट चुकी हूँ मैं

प्यार में टूट चुकी हूँ मैं
हाँ खुद से रूट चुकि हूँ मैं
नही विश्वास अब किसी पे
न एतवार किसी पे करना है ।।।

खुद के टूटे दिल को अब
खुद ही एक करना है
गलती मुझसे हुई थी
प्यार का क्या दोष इसमें
कल फिर मिलूँगी किसी हसीं ख्वाब से
बस दिल में ये आरमान है
कही तो होगा कोई तो होगा
जिसे होगा इंतज़ार मेरा

हाँ मुझे आज प्यार भी पे एतवार है
किस्मत में कुछ अच्छा होगा
इस बात का इंतेज़ार है
कल फिर होगी नयी सुबह
बस इसी का इंतज़ार है।।

Anisha Panda

She is a cute innocent girl of Odisha. She can handle every hurdles came in her life's path. Her name is Anisha Panda. Let's read her writings.

अधूरी कहानी हमारी

तेरी बातों में छुपी थी कुछ तन्हाईयाँ ,
मेरी ख़ामोशी में छुपी थी कई अर्ज़ियाँ ;
जीना चाहती थी साथ तेरे , मगर बदल गयी ज़िंदगानी हमारी ;
दुनिया से दूर तुम चली गयी और रह गया प्यार अधूरा हमारा
उस अधूरी कहानी में यादें थी कई ,
कुछ यादें खुसनुमा तोह कुछ दर्द भरी ;
खुदा का केहर है जो यूँ जुदा हुए हम ,
खुदा के आशियाने में फिर मिलेंगे हम ॥

.

मिलन जुदाई का

जुदा एक दूसरे से वह रह न सके ,
प्यार कर के भी प्यार निभा न सके ;
मिलान सम्भब नहीं पता था दोनों को ,
फिर भी अपने दिल को वह रोक न सके ;
वक़्त का यह केसा खेल है जो सामने फिर दोनों आमने सामने हैं ,
दोनों की मुश्किल वक़्त पे बने एक दूसरे के सहारे हैं ;
खोया हुआ प्यार फिर अंगड़ाई ले रही है ,
उम्मीद जो टूट गयी थी फिर एक बार जुड़ने लगी है॥

Shresth Bhargava (Yash)

Shresth Bhargava (Yash), is an emerging writer,author as well as compiler from The city of Love, The city of Taj AGRA.In his point of view , 'we can bring positive changes in the lives of peoples as well as we can ir-radicate social-evil's from our community by the help of our writings'.Apart from his writtings ,he is also a CA Aspirant ,His aim of life is to help mankind and bring positive changes in the lives of his countrymen .He has won various certificates in various competitions,He is always there for help of peoples in need .He is nature loving person,He is a devotee of Lord Shiva .He respect the ones who respects him and himself .He is verey friendly person,for him his family and friends is his lifeline
Intagram ID @yashbhargava2000

(1)

प्रवेश द्वार के पास, लंबी घास का एक ढेर।
लंबी घास के पास, लंबे तने वाले पौधे;

प्रत्येक कान झुका हुआ शंकु
तालाब की सतह पर यदि आपने बारीकी से देखा,

तुम बाहर कर सकते हैं चांदी कोई
बादल वाले तालाब के किनारे की ओर बढ़ता हुआ

जहाँ एक लड़का अपनी माँ की शर्ट में एक चौथाई के लिए रहता है।
मछली का चारा खरीदने के लिए। और उस लड़के को देख रहा है,

वह कोई अपनी हथेलियों को चूमने जाने के लिए घुटने टेक के रूप में,
मुझे याद आया कि यह कितना गूंगा होना था

उन कोइ के रूप में। मुझे लगता है कि वे शुद्ध हैं,
लड़के के हथेलियों के खाली होने के बाद भी ऐसा क्यों है,

के बाद वह देने के लिए कुछ भी नहीं था, वे अभी भी चूमा
उसके हाथ। क्योंकि जिसने ऐसा नहीं किया है-

सब कुछ होने के बाद भी बहुत प्यार से
चला गया? कोई ऐसी चीज जिसे प्यार किया हो

आप के हाथ? मुझे लगता है कि मैं अब अलग हूं।
मैं किसी भी तरह प्रबुद्ध हूं,

लेकिन मैं कौन मज़ाक कर रहा हूँ? मुझे पता है कि मैं उन लोगों की
तरह हूँ
अभी भी अपने पॉपिंग मुंह से, कि चुंबन होगा

अगर मौका दिया तो उन हाथों को फिर से। एकदम गूंगा।

Mohua Chakraborty

An optimistic doer who sees the world with rose-coloured glasses and gets visible in the introvertly emited spectra.

Rossete Of Thorns

My soul drowned as you were to leave,
Anxiously wiping my tears, I sobbed hard.
Knowing the reason behind caused my heart to cleave,
How rigid I portrayed, the thorns that slayed,
My faults were projected, broke an inch more, not to believe.
Begging to the need you should stay, I had lesions of guilt to be prayed.
Couldn't I be forgiven, and changes to be made,
Broke my rules for you, but you never valued my efforts, for you could count only the thorns of the rossete.
How easy it was for you to forget, to mock my moments,
This wasn't what I deserved, I have no more regrets.
Fragile heart and tabboos of myths and you can never hail for the rossete.

The Story Left Unnamed

Came over time, pliable to be different,
I got a 'thanks' for my enraged swipe.
Swarming thoughts moved the course,
Gapping us apart enough though.
Heavens perpetuated us to meet again,
Talk our heads out to feel what began.
Just a spark of defiance ruined the acussed,
Without relevance of dreams to be mute.
Deep down the throb, 'Bood'up' was no more an acquaintance
.
Deviated from read chapters, solely consumed with torture.
Energy that was assaulted, left the story unnamed for
dwellers.

पुलिन भारती

ये पुलिन भारती हैं। जो पेशे से सिविल इंजीनियर हैं पर दिल से एक कवि। जन्म तो पटना,बिहार में हुआ लेकिन बड़े हुए पंचग्राम, असम में।

इनकी लिखने की कला अपने आप में एक अलग पहचान है जो कई विषयों पर है।

अभी तक इनकी कविताएं इनकी डायरी तक ही सीमित थी अब ये उन(कविताओं) को दुनिया से परिचय करवा रहे हैं।

आप इनकी प्रेरक विचारों को इनके इंस्टाग्राम @bharti_pulin पर भी पढ़ सकते हैं।

मेरा प्यार

आज कई दिनों बाद नज़र आई वो,
आज फिर से तन्हाइयों में जैसे छाई वो,
उसे देख कर बस तड़प सकता हूँ मैं,
उसकी यादों को याद कर के रो ही सकता हूँ मैं।

कई दफा सवाल खुद से पूछता हूँ,
क्या उसके काबिल मैं बिल्कुल भी नही हूँ?
दिल अक्सर ही सोचते सोचते रो पड़ता है,
आखिर क्यों उसे देख कर हर बार तड़पता है??

मुझे नफरत सी हो गयी है खुद से,
आखिर कैसे आ पाऊंगा बाहर इस दुख से?
वो तो तन्हाइयों में मुझे छोड़ चली गयी,
पर क्यों कर रहा ये दिल आज भी उससे यू वफ़ाई?

Shristi Singh

She is a first year student & She started writing way back in 2016.She needs your love and support. Follow her in Instagram : shristi___singh__ and to read her works and poetries.

Be-Dard Ishq

Na door hai ishq ki
Humare haaton mein,
Na chalta ab iss dil pe
Khud ka zor hai!
Kitna ajeeb hai na yeh ishq
Ahista ahista torta hai dil,
Bina kisi shor k!
Dard se bhara hua,Dard mein lipta hua,
Fir bhi najane kyu,
Be-dard sa hai yeh ishq.

(2)

Khamosi mein bhi
Shor hai,
Tum raat k andhere mein
Jagh kar toh dekho
Be-dardi mein bhi dard nazar ayega
Tum ishq karke toh dekho!
Aakho mein aasu lekar bhi
Hooton se muskuroage
Tum dard mein hokar bhi,
Ishq mein,
Ek sukoon sa paaoge.

Aditi Vinod Patil

Myself Aditi Vinod Patil from Bangalore,I am a teacher by profession,artist by hobby, Dancer and writer by passion.
I believe there are only two ways to express our feelings,one with our words and other with our actions.So I would love to express my feelings and happiness by dancing to my own tune and to pen down my own thoughts..

Pyar Ke Side Effects

Dil diya hai Dard liya hai, yeh khuda is pyar me..
Na jaane kitne khwaab sajaaye the, tere sang jeene me..
Par lagta hai wo saare sacch honge sirf sapnon ki duniya me..
Dil diya hai Dard liya hai yeh khuda is pyar me..

Dil diya hai dard liya hai yeh khuda is pyar me..
Tut gaye saare sapne dard ke is raaha me..
Chod gaye saare apne tadapne dekte raaho me..
Dil diya hai dard liya hai yeh khud is pyar me..

Kiya wafa toh mili bewafa dard ke is raho me..
Yaad aaye saare pal Jab khoye unke khayaalon me..
Dil de kar tut gaye hum dard ke is pyar me..
Dil diya hai dard liya hai yeh khuda is pyar me..

(2)

Beintehaa mohabbat karne ka yeh matlab nahi ki hum aapki har baat maanle
Beintehaa mohabbat karne ka yeh matlab nahi ki hum aapki har baat maanle
Humne aapse bepanah Ishq karke apna dil khoya hai apna aatma-samaan nahi....

Apne kyun bohat dhoor chale jaate hai...
Jaate bhi ho toh waapas kyun nahi aate hai?
Agar Jaana hi ho toh sab kuch leke jaate...
Par apne yaadein kyun chod jaate hai?

Mehfil mein tanha hai hum aapki yaadon mein khoye hai hum
Mehfil mein tanha hai hum aapki yaadon mein khoye hai hum
Kya bataye aapko ki kaise hai hum
Bas itna samjh lo aapke bina toh zinda laash hai hum....

Dhur le jayegi humko
Yeh ruswai tumhari
Yaad karte rehna phir
Woh mulakaate humari...

Shobha Rajpal

hindi is divine. She feels quite comfortable with hindi rather english as she loves her mother tongue. She is Hindi graduated and teacher by profession.

बेदर्द इश्क:

ना मैं हँसती हूं ना वो हंसाता है
मैं रोती हू वो ना चुप कराता है
मैं मांगती हूँ वो कुछ ना दिलाता है
मैं चलती हूँ वो ना चल पाता है
मैं रुकती हूँ वो चला जाता है कहने पर कहाँ कुछ सुन पाता है
क्युकि वो इश्क नही बेदर्द है हाँ बड़ा बेदर्द है वो इश्क ही बेदर्द है।

Smriti Kumari

Smriti kumari is student by profession,writer by passion.she lives in Delhi,India. She is 2nd year student, pursuing bsc(h) maths from Rajdhani college,Delhi University. She is very passionate, inquisitive and hardworking for her work.The pen is a strong weapon for her to portray her feelings.let's enjoy her writing.

बेदर्द इश्क

बेदर्द सी ज़िन्दगी, बेदर्द -ए -जज़्बात है।
बेदर्द इश्क़ में भी मुकम्मल-ए-एहसास है।
बेदर्द सी उसकी यादें,हजारों ख्वाहिशों के साथ है।
बेदर्द ही तो है वो,जिसके लिए आज भी प्यार है।
बेदर्द है ये मौसम ,अगर उसका नहीं साथ है।
बेदर्द है ये नदियां,उसकी कश्ती जब नहीं साथ है।
बेदर्द सी ज़माने में उसके लिए कैसे पनपा प्यार है?
बेदर्द सी है ये गालियां,जब उसके आने का नहीं इंतजार हो।
बेदर्द है ये आकाश भी,अब टिमटिमाते तारों में ना वो बात हो।
बेदर्द है ये ज़माना,जिसके कारण मेरी ख्वाहिशें दरकिनार है।
बेदर्द है ये वादियां, जब उसके हाथों में ना हाथ है।
बेदर्द सी मेरी पायल की शोर,अब इसके खनखन में ना वो बात है।
बेदर्द है मेरी सूरमा, अब इसमें नहीं नशे सी बात है
सिर्फ बेदर्द नहीं मयखाना, इसमें जो सुकून-ए-एहसास है।

Pragya Verma

Pragya Verma is from Prayagraj, Uttar Pradesh. She is currently pursuing Bachelor's in Computer Application from Ewing Christian College, Prayagraj. She is a poet and a writer. Her words are her weapon to master her passion.

कुछ यूं टूटा है यह दिल

कुछ यूं टूटा है यह दिल,
कि जोड़ पाना हो गया है मुश्किल।

उसकी हर एक बातें जो चुभी हैं,
कैसे कहूं कितना दर्द देती हैं।

मेरे दो तरफे इश्क को,
एक तरफा बनाया है उसने,
इल्ज़ाम तो बहुत बड़ा लगा है उसपे,
मगर सज़ा दिया नहीं जाएगा मुझसे।

उसके गुनाह की सज़ा मुझको मिली है,
बेवफ़ाई उसने की, मगर तन्हाई मुझे मिली है।
इस इश्क की गलियों में दर्द बहुत है,
हंसना है शुरू में, फिर रोना बहुत है।

Feeling of Heartbreak

This feeling of heartbreak,
Is above of all the aches.
You left me when I needed you,
Your poison turned me blue.

You only run after the body,
You can't love somebody.
I'm shedding my tears for you,
I'm blaming myself for what you do.

Loving the bad person gives you pain,
I promise myself I wouldn't do this again.
This time will surely pass away,
And I will make a better way.

All I know about you is you're heartless,
Who left me with this much loneliness.

Sachin Banoudhiya

He is a student of Bsc

A Struggling Writter now Started Getting so many platforms

He Loves to do Audio Poetries & video Editing .

He's a Publish Co - author in so many Anthologies

Kya Yehi Thi Wo Wajah

Kya yehi thi wo Wajah
Jiske chakkr me uspar Dil laga baitha tha.
Usko apne Dil m rakh kuch is kadr khwaab buna Krta tha.
Har pal hr waqt sirf usi ki yaad m khoya rhta tha.
Uski apni Zindagi maan baitha tha.
Sb kuch sahi chal raha tha
Main use messege Karta Wo mujhe
Main Use yaad krta or
Shayad Wo bhi mujhe
Din Raat Sirf Ek msg ka Rehta tha intezaar .
Kya ye sirf dosti thi ya fir pyaar.
The phle ek normal se Friend.
Hi hello Or Fir The End..
Pr baat badi aage
Zindagi ki daud m kuch is kdr bhaage .
Time nikalna hua uske liye mushkil
Time to saala Mere Paas bhi nhi tha.
Pr pta nhi kese Main he Kyu nikal leta tha.
Aksar Dil lagaye baitha
Wait krta tha keval uske msg ke reply ko.
Uske liye Kayi baar ignore kiya apne Friends even apne Bhai ko.
Kayi promises kiye shayd sabhi nibhaye bhi.
Pr Kya yehi wo wajh thi
Jo ek bhi kaam aaye nahi.

Arijit Mondal

Arijit Mondal ,a boy with big dreams. He is very much hardworking and energetic guy and a reliable friend to hand around. He is a bookaholic in nature and loves to pen down his feelings. He believes hardwork is the major key to success .

What do you say this ?

Hey , you , listen...
I don't know who you are ,
Even I don't know who am I talking to ,
You are there in my heart ,
I cannot touch you .
But I can feel you ,
And express that feeling on my notebook .
We both exist in one self .
My heartbeat doubles when I think of you .
When I call you by name ,
it seems as if ,
my heart is no longer with me ,
It is gone to you .
Well !! What do you say this ?

Heartbeat

The word "heartbeat" is as deep as it is easy to say .Not everyone will understand it .

This will be understood by those who could not propose to the people they love and with whom they meet every day .They both understand better who proposed and who have been proposed .One who had committed suicide but couldn't do can feel "Heartbeat" better .If you have already faced any interview , then you have a clear vision about it .He/she also knows very well what "Heartbeat" is who have watched moron cup .

In the end, it is such a feeling that cannot be expressed in words .

Oke Damilola Deborah

Damilola is a 19 year old Nigerian writer.She started writing in the year 2016 as a hobby.She is so excited to have some of her work published.

Away

Fallen to the ground and casted away by the wind to a place dry and bereaved.
Gently you moved, dancing to the sound,a sound lovely to the ear but dangerous to the mind.
You never stopped till you were away to lost.
So away that you missed your road back to us.
Back to home,back to where you are loved.

Splitter

LIke a crash my emotions was thrown to the wall and scattered on the ground.
Left and can't be packed because they were like sand.
Don't blame me if I act the opposite It's just that I now lack feelings.
Not my fault but your fault.
You should have been more careful with my emotions as you would while holding an egg,
Maybe now it would have been a different story shared.

Goodbye

We were 'in' love but, love sent us parking.
Since love was the only shelter we both shared, having been thrown out by love,now we have to go our ways apart in search of a new shelter.
Love in our case threw us far apart,and all left of us is our past to tell.
Bet it's a goodbye.

Mihika Saraf

Mihika Saraf is an aspiring 12 year old poet and author. She enjoys writing poetry, novels, quotes, articles and motivational speeches. She is a published poet and co-author. She has been author of the year 2019 nominee and 1st place holder (best poet from 4-7 std category) in SSWC contest, both held by storymirror app. Most of her writings and accomplishments are displayed on the same. She aims to grow of vocabulary and develop for her readers, an interest in diverse topics.

I Still Remember You

I talk to myself about you,

As tears roll and I feel my veins freeze,

Even my hues and blues think about you,

As my numbness isolates the breeze.

The warmth of your touch I still feel,

As I remember us walking ashore,

I also remember your comforting laugh honey,

Which makes me think of you much much more.

And I still step up the stairs,

To see if you're sleeping above,

Yet I'm unable to feel that your soul is peaceful,

So, today I'm jumping down- in the hope to find your love...

Vishal Agrawal

He was born and brought up in mathura uttar pradesh. He is engineering student pursuing his bachelor's degree from GLA university mathura. He is multi talented and multi tasker. He likes singing, skeching and writing. he writes to expresses his feeling and emotions on the paper. Sometimes his quotes and shayri inspire and motivate people. He feels that his hardwork is his biggest strength. He is co-author of 15+ books which also include vajra world record holder anthology.he is compiler of 3 books: The mysterious life, Verses of life and My Country My pride

जो इन्साफ की बात करते थे वो आज गुन्हेगार बन गए

जो बफा, इश्क़, मोहब्बत की बात करते थे
वो आज बफादार ना रहे,
जो इन्साफ की बात करते थे
वो आज गुन्हेगार बन गए,

कहते थे तुमसे इश्क़ दिल से करते हैं
वो आज दिलदार ना रहे,
जो इन्साफ की बात करते थे
वो आज गुन्हेगार बन गए,

शायद यही परिणाम है, इश्क़ का
अपने थे वो अपने ना रहे,
जो बदनामी से डरते थे
आज वो खुद बदनाम हो गए,

किसी ने सदा के लिये तो किसी ने कुछ पल के लिये किया
खुद को इस गम का हिस्सेदार कह गए,
जो सारे जहाँ की बात करते थे
वो मुसाफिर थे मुसाफिर रह गए,
जो इन्साफ की बात करते थे
वो आज गुन्हेगार बन गए,,

Sanya Khanna

Sanya is someone who always manages to create a positive aura around her. She is constantly smiling without complaining much about the difficulties. She is confident in whatever she does and is very hardworking. She has never learnt to give up in life. Whatever the situation maybe, she completes all the tasks given to her on time and in an organised manner. She has keen interest in writing and has been a part of various anthologies. She is extremely friendly and manages to work well in a team and that is her greatest strength!

"Our Love Was Beautiful"

It always breaks my heart,
Seeing you this apart!
Who once meant the world to me,
Is now just a part of history..

You always promised to be together
Like the birds of same feather..
Then what made you go so far,
Forgetting all the promises we made under the shooting star?

I gave my everything to you,
Still how smoothly you had bid me adieu!
Giving me false hopes of meeting again
Knowing it would just intensify my pain..

Your love was like a rainbow,
Pleasing but went away with the flow!
Even today my heart aches remembering the drives,
we had under the blue-skies!

I wonder if you still miss me,
Our love was beautiful, can we please agree??

Neha Singhania

Hello, introducing Neha Singhania. She is Pursuing CS and she is a good dancer. Writing is her passion, and she want to be a good known writter.she always try to write on undefined feelings.. she having her own instagram page @ dil-e-ehsasss.

Perfect Us

In a dark room
m sitting alone,
thinking about you and
the time that we spent together
the memories that we cheered upon and
the fun that we had,
the way you always cared for me,
your unexpressed feelings for me,
And my unshown secret love for you
then suddely,
your pictures hits me hard
i am broken down and torn
i am crying more
it feels like m dying
it feels m nothng
because you complete me baby
missing our endlesstalks, sleppless nights
you were the jar of my happiness and joy.
i am alone even surrouding with many people
you! Yes only you m missing through out my day and night..
you have a place in my heart like no one else could ever
have.
Because you are the one perfect for me..
that's what I really feel after our breakup.

Aditya Srivastava

Aditya is a future engineer. He had also been part a of 10+ anthologies and writes when he desires to.He wants to make his career in research field and wants to find something great for the good cause of the world.

You can connect to him at: @b.e.z.u.b.a.n__d.i.l

Bewafa Nikli Wo

Ye garmi ke mousam me

Itni barsaat kyu ho rahi hai

Or jise ishq kiya beinteha

Aaj wahi imtehaan le rahi hai

Par na use chor sakta hu

Or na hi wo mere sath rehti hai

Or kehne ko kuch bhi nahi

Bas itna hai

Ki meri jannat jaise zindigi ka

Janaja uth gaya

Or wo bas yun hi dhire dhire karke

Meri jaan le rahi hai.

Chirag L Sagar

Chirag L Sagar is a 1st year MBBS student studying at Srinivas Institute of Medical Sciences and Research Centre,Mangalore. His hobbies are poetry, reading - books,novels, autobiographies,philately, listening to songs,sports like cricket and badminton,cooking. He is a medico by profession and a writer by passion. His best friend Nihar,has always been his inspiration and motivation to do great in whatever he does. His dream is to become an Oncologist and a successful writer.

Instagram : @chirag_cls18 Facebook : Chirag LSagar

I'm broken

Why did you choose to tear me apart,

When I wasn't in a position to recover ?

Has there been any mistake from my side,

That you're punishing me so badly.

You broke my trust deep inside my wounded heart.

Why did you have to select me,

To shatter my dreams forever ?

Wasn't I worthy of your love,

That you'd to ditch me for someone unknown person.

If that's the case, and is true,

Then first of all,

Why did you opt to fall in love with me ?

Maitreyee

She is Maitreyee. Don't go by her age since she can bemuse you with her words! She is bubbly, scintilating and ambitious. She has expertise in story telling, micro tales and also weaving words into beautiful poetries. Apart from this she is a foodie and also loves cooking.

Just Another..

You're just another dream,

Just another love story gone to waste,

Just another poem to go

In my collection of what-could-have-been fate.

You could have been my guy,

But now you've made me cry.

You could have been the one,

But, unfortunately, we're done

I had liked you from a far,

Not my fault you stole my heart,

Then we hung out more and more,

But now, my heart is sore.

I was happy around you,

I didn't know I could feel like this too,

But, as all sad endings express,

It turned out too good to be true.

I give up! I quit!

There's just no use anymore.

Because of you, now we're through,

And Love and I are now in war.

You made me happy,

I thought a fairy-tale ending could happen to me,

Or at least, a happy ending,

But not even that seems allowed for me.

I spill my heart out on these poems,

Or, at least, what little still remains,

I might as well anyway.

There's not a guy that would take my heart and all its pain.

So here I am, shedding my tears,

Wasting away over you,

Who now is nothing but a memory,

Another reason why love is what I fear.

It hurts so much,

It fails so often,

Is being happy,Now a sin?

I told myself you wouldn't,

I hoped that you would never be,

A memory etched on paper,

Just another piece of poetry.

Soumya Nema

A lawyer for cases and a non judgemental judge for humanity, Soumya Nema is a observer and consequent writer at core. Different delicacies and new places charge her up to smile all day and she is fond of reading and analysing only to ponder and pour out the best

बेपरवाह सी वो जब किसी कहानी के अक्स को पन्नों पर उकेरती है उसकी और अल्फाजों की गुफ्तगू भी जनाब हर बार एक हसीन आरजू सी लगती है...

" वो मैं थी"

नहीं पता मुझे

बस आज कुछ टूटा सा है

मेरे ख्यालों की कायनात में ये कैसी बारिश है

जो ना थम रही है ना रुक रही है

नहीं पता मुझे

बस अब थमना चाहती हूं संभालना चाहती हूं

दिल की आवाज बहुत सुन चुकी, अब धड़कनों को रोकना चाहती हूं

दिल की इस बंधी डोर को अब काटना चाहती हूँ

मिन्नतें हजार की, ख्वाहिशें हजार थी

पर शायद मुकम्मल ना कर पाई अपने फासलों को

एक हाथ तो था पर दूजा, शायद भीड़ उसे दिखा ना पाई

आज भी वही एहसास है बस उसे बता ना पाई

आहिस्ता -आहिस्ता ही सही, अब मैंने उसे सुनना बंद कर दिया है

आहिस्ता-आहिस्ता ही सही ये सफर भी आसान हो जाएगा

फिर ना ये दिल रहेगा ना ये दर्द

आहिस्ता -आहिस्ता ही सही, पता चल गया

जो टूटा था वो कोई खिलौना नहीं

" वो मैं थी"

Tushar Sachdeva

12th grade student , love to write shayaris..

। बीते लमहे ।

वो समहा भी कुछ हसीन था ,
जब तू मेरे करीब था
जान वारते थे एक दूजे के वास्ते
फिर कयो अलग हुए हमारे रास्तो ?
तू ही खुदा मेरा ,
तुझसे ही मेरी खुदाई थी
फिर क्या वजह बनी इस जुदाई की ?

अब जुदा हो ही चुके हों
तो यूं ही मुसकराते रहना
था सफर खूबसूरत अपना
याद दिलाते रहना..

अब आदत नही तेरे साथ की
तेरे संग बिताई हर मुलाकात की
पर तेरी फिक्र हर लम्हे मैं करता हूँ
वैसे तो शायर नहीं ,

पर तेरा जिक्र हर पन्हे में करता हूँ ..

याद आती है सारी शामें ,

जो बिताइ तेरे नाम

तू सही या मैं गलत

नाजाने किस पर है ये सारे इल्जाम

माना कुछ परेशानियां जरूर होगी

कुछ कमी तो मुझमे भी जरूर होगी

बीते हुए पलों का दर्द फिल्हाल जरूर रहेगा

मैं काबिल था या नही ये सवाल जरूर रहेगा

Tusar Ranjan Mahapatra

Very enthusiastic and fun-loving. Engineer by profession, writer and musician by passion, he loves to try out new things just for the sheer fun of it. He loves life and everything and everyone in it.

A Thing No More

So we are no more a thing
No longer does my name brighten u up
No longer do u smile thinking of me
No longer do our lovely memories come
When we think of us
So we are no more a thing
My mind punishes me
For even thinking about u
Every touch that I made
Makes me feel like a molester
Every talk we exchanged
Makes me question our integrity
So we are no more a thing
For every thought
Involving "us"
Now ignites a fire so deep
Pumping me to work
To better myself
To make myself
To be equal to someone
Just like u
Coz we are no more a thing
And I don't know who fell short
So I ain't left with a choice
But to live with "our" dreams
To fulfil them for all they are worth
As we are a thing no more...

For None

It was all but for none
All the happiness for none
All the sadness for none
It was all but for none
The laughter was for none
The smiles were for none
The sleepless nights lost
The merciless thoughts were for none
For all that was for you
You thought to be for none
For all that I did for only you
You deemed it for none
As the world sees me for me
Maybe for you I was none
As my deeds used to be for all
Maybe you thought it was for none
Failed to see the attachment
Fault was mine, of else none
Failed to understand me perhaps
Fault was mine, of else none
Now all that's left of me
Can be nurtured by none
Now the heart that beats within me
Cannot beat anymore for none
Now the dreams that haunt me
Caress my mind for none
For now, all that lives of me
Does so for you and only you
Cares more or thinks more for none

Bushra Shaikh

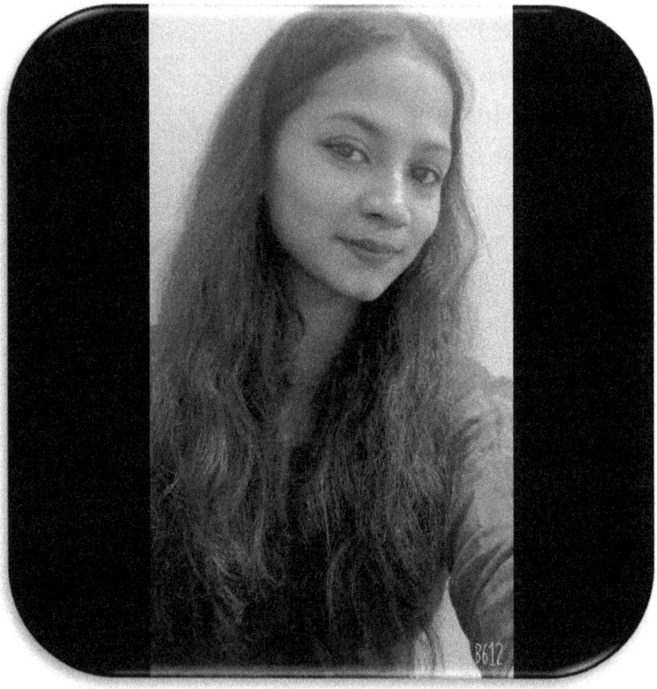

Bushra Shaikh is a 21-year-old girl from Mumbai. She is studying physiotherapy. She likes to read and write. She is good at sports as well.

Dill Toota

Dil toota hi sahi par pass toh hai
Ishq adhura hi sahi par uske ehsaas sath toh hai
Sath chhuta hi sahi par uske khayal sath toh hai
Dil toota hi sahi par pass toh hai

Dr. Ruchita Chauhan

Hye there!
Her name is Dr. Ruchita Chauhan.
She is a Dentist by Profession and Writer by Passion.
She merely loves to express her feelings by penning down the feels of her soul.
Hence she quoted " I FEEL, I WRITE".
The emotions of her soul that she pours out make others find it relatable to the tale of their lives and ultimately touches the core of their heart.
Pursuing passion and profession concurrently bestows peace to an inner piece of her.
Admin of The Real Thoughts

Inner Wound

A gossiping girl has become a hushed soul.
Her gracious heart is now a prisoner of her mind.
Her potency has ended up in her vulnerability.
She commenced sneaking her tears faking giggles.
She started drowning in the memories, they had created once.
Her possessiveness has turned out into fragility.
Her devotion has become poisonous for her.
A girl who used to live has turned on just surviving.
Her trust has ended her up into the worst and her inner self is just not as fine as outer self anymore just because the soul wound has shaped her.

Recovery From Heartbreak

That day will certainly come.

When you yourself will be self-standing proudly.
You will be extremely delighted and
no one would have their restraint on it.

Nothing will ever dominate you anymore.
Neither you will be bounded by the memories nor by forged
people in fact the abundant peace will wrap you around.

You will not be frightened of losing anyone.
Your bursts will turn into giggles
and your nightmares will convert into the dreams.

Those bad times won't gain come any day, nothing will hit
you emotionally nor mentally.

Indeed, it will take time but trust the universe.
It will surely bring you a day when you will be recovered...

Saheb Ghosh

Saheb Ghosh, a frankly fellow to everyone, he consummately believes in God's existence. He is a righteous person who likes simplicity. He writes poems and short stories in an easy language both in English and Bengali.

Real Love Can Never Be Forgotten

I hope that now you are very happy as you are not bound before me. Those days are now converted into memories. When you were present before me, I had much cared you and excessively loved you and incessantly tried to make you happy. Your every unfulfilled desires I had fufilled in a wink, but I was failed to recognise your deceiving mind and selfishness. Today we are separated but till now I have love for you because I was loved you from my heart, not from my brain and till now my heart beat hail the name of you. Your cunningness never gave me the value of my love but I know you will not forget me because you know how much I love you. Though we are now in long distance but I had loved you, I love you and I will love you era after era.

Immature Love

I have to convey a stain
Which you've given me,
And it will remain as a pain;
In my heart it will be throbbing.

The proposal, I had made,
In your eyes it seems an infatuation.
I, first had tried to express my emotion,
But you said you never think so.

That day your words made me fie;
You just said, you see me as a friend.
But I thought you something else in my life, for that
I wanted to sacrifice myself in your hands.

Flairs & Glairs

Flairs and Glairs, a platform by a student for the students. We are esteemed youth struggling to carve out our path for our future and we follow a basic mindset Since everyone is not born with all-round skills. Joining hands with people who are born to execute it with perfection is the best way to evolve. Self-Evolution is the need of the hour but, evolving as a community is what we strive for. The initiative as kickstarted by, Founder- Mr. Shubham Shah with the motive to utilize the skillset and talent of writing has now a team of 10+ people who are actively participating into newer forms of learning and discovering talents among youngsters. We Provide platform and services like Publishing opportunities, Open mics, Workshops, Hands-on training. Operating with Brand Name Of Flairs and Glairs (Publication House), we offer the chance of elevating a passionate writer to an esteemed author With Brand name Teekhe Zasbaaat, We bring to you an opportunity to get accustomed with the Public Speaking and Presenting of Thoughts along with regular challenges to brush up your inking spirit. The newest initiative to extend our services we introduced in a new writing Platform- The Glittering Fables and Ink Over Tears.

We Choose to Fly Like A Falcon than to be a

Leg Pulling Crab.

To Know More: Infoline – 7781900870
Mail Us At-
flairsandglairs@gmail.com / info@flairsandglairs.in
Or Visit is at
www.flairsandglairs.com / www.flairsandglairs.in
Social Handles- @flairsandglairs @teekhezasbaaat

www.ingramcontent.com/pod-product-compliance
Lightning Source LLC
Chambersburg PA
CBHW050529240926
51846CB00003B/747
* 9 7 8 9 3 9 0 4 1 6 8 9 9 *